Travel and
transport

THIS BLOOMSBURY BOOK

BELONGS TO

....

KU-213-437

For Sophie Short
S.G.

For Nick, Daniel and Alexander,
and all the mums and children who'll have
fun together playing with this book . . .
B.V.

Bloomsbury Publishing, London, Berlin, New York and Sydney

First published in Great Britain in July 2011 by Bloomsbury Publishing Plc
36 Soho Square, London, W1D 3QY

Text copyright © Sally Grindley 2011
Illustrations copyright © Barbara Vagnozzi 2011
The moral rights of the author and illustrator have been asserted

A CIP catalogue record of this book is available from the British Library

ISBN 978 1 4088 0036 2

1 3 5 7 9 10 8 6 4 2

MIX
Paper from
responsible sources
FSC® C003532
FSC www.fsc.org

Printed in China by Toppan Leefung Printing Ltd, Dongguan, Guangdong

www.bloomsbury.com

Tin

Dee

Busy Day

Jack

Rose

Sally Grindley

Illustrated by

Barbara Vagnozzi

Harry

Rafa

BLOOMSBURY

LONDON BERLIN NEW YORK SYDNEY

'There's a hole in this tyre,' a mechanic tells Tin.
While he fixes the tyre, a blue tanker drives in.

They set off again and the bus picks up speed.
A big yellow combine is harvesting seed.

I want to drive one of those!

There's a tractor ahead with a trailer of hay.

A loud noise above makes them look at the sky.
It's a green helicopter – would you like to fly?

A bright orange digger is blocking the road.

They come to a halt as it lifts up its load.

The grey dumper truck is stuck in the mud.
At last it pulls free with a clunk and a thud.

The bus travels fast. The friends sing a song.
They bounce up and down as they rumble along.

Then, quick as a flash, Dee leaps from her seat.
'The sea!' she cries out. Now they're all on their feet.

They run to the beach when at last the bus stops, and watch a hang-glider swoop from the cliff tops.

That looks scary.

They race to the water and splash through the waves,

chase crabs around rock pools and visit the caves.

They build a huge castle with buckets of sand,

and dance to the sound of a distant brass band.

The beach is now empty. The crowds have all gone.

The red bus is waiting, its engine switched on.

They clamber aboard and before very long,
they're asleep, snoring gently.